ANGUS WILSON MCKINNON

A CONFEDERATE SOLDIER

THE MAKING OF A MAN

TOM MCKINNON

authorHOUSE®

AuthorHouse™
1663 Liberty Drive
Bloomington, IN 47403
www.authorhouse.com
Phone: 1 (800) 839-8640

Published by AuthorHouse   10/14/2015

ISBN: 978-1-5049-5566-9 (sc)
ISBN: 978-1-5049-5565-2 (e)

DEDICATION

This book is dedicated to my children, Anna Laura, Lisa Carol, Thomas Alexander and all of the hundreds of other McKinnon's descended from Angus.

Contents

ANGUS WILSON McKINNON

Angus was born in Alabama, Tallapoosa County, on December 11, 1844. His parents were William Alexander "Sandy" McKinnon and Sarah Cameron McKinnon both born in North Carolina in 1806. They were married May 12, 1831 after their families had moved to Walton County, Georgia. About 1840 after the birth of their fourth children, the young family moved to Tallapoosa County, Alabama where Angus was born. Angus was next to the youngest of seven children. In approximately 1855, when Angus was 11 years old, the family made their final move to Union County in Arkansas.

William Alexander was a substance farmer and, perhaps seeking to escape the plantation system, established a farm in new territory in Western Union County, Arkansas. Several Scottish families moved together including the Cameron's, McGoogan's and others. They became members of the newly established Scotland Presbyterian Church.

Angus grew up on the farm. They worked hard to clear the land and cultivated crops of corn for corn meal as well as feeding livestock. Cotton was raised for much needed cash. They raised virtually all their food on the farm. It was a life of hard work and Angus fully participated. By his 17th birthday he felt ready to strike out on his own. Over his mother's objections he joined the newly established Confederate Army. This is where this story begins.

FOREWORD

I've written this story to record for future generations the civil war experiences of Angus McKinnon, my great grandfather. This account seeks to give the view of the war from Angus' perspective. Historical documentation is rather sketchy. Since no one can know his specific feelings except for the actions he took, I have fictionalized thoughts and words based on the true locations, battles, and his travels. True names of the individuals are cited but again I used fictional tools to bring their personalities to life.

This is a work of fiction. However, each chapter is preceded with corresponding historical account of the major events of the war. I visited the sites of the major battles to try to gain some understandings for the events that Angus experienced. I stood on the very battlefields where Angus witnessed the horrors of war and the strength of friendship. I can only perceive the fear, excitement, and final disillusionment that Angus must have felt. Today these battlegrounds feel so tranquil and beautiful, I find it hard to image the suffering and tragic loss of life that occurred more than 150 years ago.

Researching the history of Angus proved frustrating. As is often the case, records and dates do not always agree. For instance, the census records of 1870 and 1880 have him born in 1844 but the census of 1860 list his birth date as 1842. His monument in the Scotland cemetery has 1840 as his date of birth. The monument was erected at a later date to replace the original marker that can no longer be read.

The actual dates of his military service are also unclear. My first source was written by Bryan R. Howerton who researched the roster of Company C of the 2nd Arkansas Infantry. He states that Angus W. McKinnon was in the 2nd infantry; wounded at the Battle of Mechanicsville or Beaver Dam Creek on June 16, 1862; transferred to Company G of the 3rd Arkansas Infantry; discharged July 18, 1862; and later joined Company G of the 8th Louisiana Calvary. Other records show that the 8th Louisiana Calvary was not organized until 1864 and that roster does not include Angus McKinnon.

Official records of the National Archives show that he was transferred to Company G, 3rd Arkansas Infantry on July 18, 1862 but has no record of his service after that date. However, the official records include an application by Eliza Jane McKinnon, his widow, for a pension in 1901 after Angus' death. The proof of service part of the application states the he served from October, 1861 to May, 1865. The application for a grant of $50 was endorsed by J. B. Robertson and L. H. Sheppard, prominent citizens at the time.

So I have three alternative scenarios. First, he was discharged in 1862 returned home and joined the 8th Louisiana Calvary in 1864. Second, the official archives have him in the 3rd Arkansas infantry but never mentioned that he was discharged or any further campaigns. Third, a possible error was made that has him in the 8th Louisiana Calvary instead the 8th Louisiana Infantry which was in the area when he was discharged and they went on to fight numerous battles. The roster of the 8th Louisiana Infantry includes only those who originally joined it.

The manner in which battle names were assigned and the related battle records are also confusing. The Union command generally named the battles for a stream while the Confederates named them for a nearby town. Consequently, for example, the Battle of Beaver Dam Creek is also known as the Battle of Mechanicsville, the Battles of Manassas as Bull Run and the Battle Antietam as Sharpsville.

Based on my research and logical thinking I conclude that it is most plausible that Angus was born in 1844 and served in the 8th Louisiana Infantry.

Angus McKinnon Confederate Soldier

The Beginnings

Arkansas like the other Border States of Tennessee, North Carolina and Virginia, did not vote to secede when the first secession convention was called March 17, 1861. But after Fort Sumter was fired on and Abraham Lincoln called for troops from Arkansas to fight the Rebels, the Governor quickly called a second convention on May 16, 1861. The Arkansas delegates voted to secede. Some delegates from Northern Counties voted no. When it passed, the chair asked for a unanimous vote. All but Isaac Murphy from Madison County voted "yes." The state responded rapidly to the perceived Unionist threat. Military units were organized in all parts of the state.

Among the first was the 1st Arkansas Infantry regiment organized in Southeast Arkansas and the 3rd Arkansas Infantry in South Central Arkansas. A company from Three Creeks, Union County, was included in the 3rd. The two new Arkansas Infantry Regiments were sent to Virginia in June and July. In September the 1st Regiment sent some officers back to Arkansas to recruit additional units.

Three voluntary companies were organized in El Dorado, Pine Bluff, and Hot Springs to join the 1st Regiment. The three companies were hastily sent to Virginia where the Confederate War Department decided that their addition to the 1st would make it too large. Consequently, they became the 2nd Arkansas Infantry Battalion. Angus McKinnon was a private in Company C, the El Dorado Company that named itself the "Fagan Rifles" after Colonel James Fleming Fagan of the 1st Regiment.

The first assignment of Company C was patrolling the southern shores of the Potomac River. A large number of the company were ill with dysentery as well of other ailments that winter. Several died. The first combat they saw was the Battle of Beaver Dam Creek or Mechanicsville.

CHAPTER 1

Angus felt both fear and excitement. He was surrounded by his buddies who had been with him since they all joined the Confederate Army last September back in Arkansas. Company C of the 2nd Arkansas Infantry or "Fagan's Rifles" as they called themselves, was approaching the Yankee entrenchment on the other side of Beaver Dam Creek in Virginia. They had been camped in a defensive position for several weeks but the new General of the Army of Northern Virginia, Robert E Lee, now gave the order to attack.

Suddenly a shot rang out and Sergeant Parnell yelled, "Charge." The Confederates broke into a run and the rebel yell echoed across the draw. It was total chaos. Men fired, stopped to reload and, running, fired again. Angus for the first time saw fellow soldiers being hit and falling to the ground bleeding. Some cried out but others were deathly still. But he couldn't stop. Urged on by Sergeant Parnell, he jumped over fallen comrades and

continued his charge toward the enemy. The bullets were flying on all sides. Smoke made it hard to see the enemy. Suddenly Angus was knocked to the ground and couldn't understand why. Then he felt wetness spreading across his left shoulder and blacked out.

Angus woke up with a terrible pain along his left side and shoulder. "Where was he?" He heard groans and moans on all sides and intermittent anguished screams. The prevailing acrid smells were mixed with the metallic smell of blood and human excrement. As Angus turned his head, he saw that he was lying on a ragged piece of canvas on the ground surrounded by a host of other wounded.

An older man whom he assumed to be a doctor briefly examined his shoulder and pronounced that his wound was not life threatening. It seemed that the mini ball had lost most of its momentum when it struck him and was lodged in his left shoulder resulting in profuse bleeding but nothing more serious than a broken rib. His treatment would wait on the more seriously wounded.

Angus thought that if it was not so serious, he could remove the bullet himself. He stuck a finger in the wound seeking the mine ball but failed to find it. The resulting pain made him faint. The pain was unremitting as Angus dozed with feverous dreams of charges into the Yankee's line and mangled bodies all around. He was vaguely aware of being placed on a stretcher and moved.

When he awoke again he was surprised to find himself in a hospital bed. His shoulder was tightly bandaged but still throbbed painfully. His feverous forehead was being soothed with a wet cloth in the hands of a young woman. It felt so good and he wished she would stay but shortly she turned to the next bed in a long row of wounded men.

As Angus lay there his thoughts returned to his home on the farm in South Arkansas. He was only 17 when he left and now so far from home. Angus remembered with nostalgia the quiet days of work in the fields, the closeness of the family at the end of the day, and the wagon ride to church every Sunday. His thoughts lingered on the beautiful face of Eliza Jane Keeling. Angus was never able to approach her but he was thrilled when one Sunday after church she first said, "hello." He was smitten but too shy to talk about more than the weather and crops.

Angus was never much for politics but when Arkansas voted to leave the Union, he joined in the excitement of other young men at the church meeting. He remembered how Colonel Fagan had sent recruiters around to local communities to rile up young men to join the army. Even though there was talk of saving the plantation culture almost none of them had slaves, and slavery was not considered to be the issue. They had to defend the homeland against the invading Yankees sent by Abraham Lincoln to destroy the Southern way of life. Angus was urged to join by his friends William Keeling, Malcom McGoogan and the Cameron boys, Bill and J. C. He was ready to go.

Angus hurried home to excitedly announce to his family that he was off to defend their home. They were much less excited.

His mother said, "No, You are not going. Your brother Thomas has already gone and we need you on the farm. I can't bear to lose two sons."

Angus pleaded his case but his mother was unrelenting until his father broke in. "The boy has to do what he thinks is right. We can all help bring in the crops."

His mother had not quite come to terms with his going but had to accept his father's decision, so she packed him a huge lunch and with a tearful hug saw him off. His Father shook his hand with an unusual squeeze and told him how proud he was.

Recruits had to travel to El Dorado, the county seat, to be inducted. Angus was to meet his four friends to join up. The sun was shining brightly as they met at the crossroads and rode their farm mules the 12 miles into El Dorado. The Cameron boys' younger brother went along to bring the mules back home.

El Dorado was a small town but the population soon swelled by the arrival of new recruits. There was general chaos. Young men milled around, venders hawked military supplies, and ladies offered lemonade to arriving recruits.

The young men were unsure as to where they should report. A well-dressed man seeing their confusion directed them to the courthouse. "Tell the sergeant that I sent you." He said.

An old sergeant was at a desk giving out papers to be signed by a line of young men to become new soldiers. When Angus and the others approached the desk, the Sargent asked if they came of their own accord. They answered "yes."

"I thought so," he said. "That old scoundrel is trying to defraud the army by collecting a stipend for bringing in new recruits."

After signing up they were directed to report to captain John Lacy at the South end of town. There they were told to fall in with about 90 other recruits to receive instructions. It was a ragged formation and the first sergeant began chewing them out in vile language beyond what the boys had ever heard. They could see that this would be quite an education. This didn't quell their excitement about the coming adventures and they fervently hoped that the war would not be over before they could get to the front line.

Despite the sounds of wounded soldiers around him, Angus dozed off. His last thought was his earlier fears of missing the action. He'd made it in plenty of time.

Angus woke up from a long sleep and felt better. His fever had abated. As he lay there he heard a familiar voice bellowing. "Where is Angus McKinnon?" He recognized the voice of John Pickering, one from his company.

Angus tried to rise as John approached and John plopped down on the side of his bed. "The Yanks can't keep you down. How the hell are you?"

Angus weakly replied, "I'll be up in a couple of days." How are Murphy, the Cameron boys, and the rest of Company C?"

John's mood abruptly changed as he replied, "Bill didn't make it and JC is around here somewhere. More than half of our boys were killed or wounded. The Yanks had to move out before they could kill anymore." Angus lay back and closed his eyes.

"We can be proud," John continued. "Here is a section of the newspaper that tells about the battle."

Regarding the 2nd Arkansas Battalion that led the charge, the <u>Richmond Dispatch</u> that tells of the battle. John cleared his voice and read the article regarding the 2nd Arkansas Battalion who led the charge:

> "These are the men who add to the name of patriot the sacred name of exile—these are the brave hearts who have answered the war-call from a distance quarter,…They were cool and determined; they looked with confidence upon the calm dauntless brow of their commander, Major Bronaugh, and hailed in their hearts the triumph yet to come… The Arkansas Battalion lost more men in proportion to its number than that of any other command. They went into the fight like men and discharged their duty bravely, and when darkness closed the conflict, Major Bronaugh (mortally wounded) was found heroically at his post with twelve men, whom he had rallied in the hottest fight."

The praise did not make Angus feel any less despondent. This cruel war had taken his comrades at their prime and cut them down. It was not the thrilling adventure that he had envisioned but a bloody nightmare. Why did they do it?

As Angus looked off in the distance, John slapped him on his good shoulder and said, "Keep it up. I'm going to look for JC."

The Virginia Campaign

In the spring of 1862 the Union Army made a concerted effort to capture the Confederate capital of Richmond and bring an end to the war. A force of 125,000 under the command of George B. McClelland landed near the mouth of the James River and rapidly moved toward Richmond. The Confederate forces under the command of Joseph E. Johnston were steadily moved back in a defensive position until the Union a

Army was within five miles of Richmond. At that point Johnston was severely wounded at the Battle of Seven Pines and President Jefferson Davis called on Robert E. Lee to take command of the Army of Northern Virginia. Lee seeing that his forces were outnumbered with inferior supplies decided that the best course of action was to attack.

The Union forces were divided by the Chickahominy River and the decision was to attack the smaller force north of the river. The Battle of Beaver Dam Creek or Mechanicsville was the beginning of the Seven Days' Battles. At the battle the 2nd Arkansas Battalion along with the 16th, 22nd and 34th North Carolina Regiments was put under the command of A. P. Hill and led the charge on the Federal's position. The Union Forces were alerted to the attack. They were dug in on the upward slopes of the creek and put down a withering fire.

Positioned at the forefront, the 2nd Arkansas was decimated. There was no official casualty list reported as there was no commissioned or non-commissioned officers left standing to make any reports. The Confederates were unable to dislodge the Union position and suffered disproportional heavy losses-1,475 Confederate killed or wounded to 361 for the Union. McClellan, hearing of the impending approach of additional Confederate forces under the command of Stonewall Jackson, was unnerved and gave the order to fall back.

Lee continued to attack in a series of battles that drove the Union Army back toward the James River. The battles were fought at Gains Mill, Savage Station, Glendale, and Malvern Hill. Even though it seemed that McClellan had the upper hand, he continued to retreat falling back to the James River. Shortly thereafter McClellan abandoned the Peninsular Campaign and the Union Forces boarded ships to sail back to Washington. At the beginning of the campaign it seemed that Richmond would fall and the war would be near an end. But McClellan's failure facilitated three more years of war.

CHAPTER 2

As Angus lay on his hospital bed, he remembered the elation he'd felt as they departed El Dorado for Pine Bluff to join the two other companies to form what was to become the 2nd battalion.

After their initial formation each member of the "Fagan Rifles" was issued a new rifle shipped up from New Orleans. The Enfield Rifles were not the most modern but excellent weapons for loading and firing rapidly. Angus remembered caressing the carved mahogany stock and smooth metal of the barrel. It was the best rifle that he had ever had in his hands. Of less interest was the issue of wool blankets and ground cloths. No uniforms were available but promised when they reached Virginia.

The next order of business was the formation of mess groups. Seven or eight of the new recruits were assigned to cook together and given a small trunk with a pot, skillet, and metal plates with spoons and forks. The plates and utensils were added to each one's bed roll.

Mess groups were generally formed by recruits who were seen hanging around together. So Angus' group included the Cameron boys and four others. Bill, the elder Cameron brother, was somewhat quiet and seemed more mature than the others in the group. In contrast, JC was loud and boisterous, ready for any adventure. Malcom McGoogan, whom Angus had known all his life, was cautious but usually went along with the group. John Pickering was outgoing and a natural leader that drew others to him. William Keeling was almost the same age as Angus and even though they were close, he was a bit standoffish. These six privates were joined by 3rd Sergeant William Brown who was capable but the others soon learned, had a drinking problem.

Even though Sergeant Brown had the senior rank, Pickering took leadership and the group was soon making a fire to cook the fat back and corn pone that they were issued for supper. After eating, Keeling put more wood on the fire and the group sat around it speculating about the future.

Sergeant Brown brought out a jar of moonshine and after taking a big swig offered to pass it around. Bill Cameron declined but the others each took a drink in turn. Being a strict Presbyterian Angus had never tasted liquor before. He found the burning sensation very unpleasant. That was the case for most of the others but they felt very worldly and were soon boasting of how they would take care of the Yankees in short order.

After a short night's sleep on the hard ground, they were rudely awakened by the first sergeant. They were given a piece of corn pone and told to pack up their gear and fall in. They made some semblance of a formation and were addressed by Captain Lacy. Company C was to proceed to Pine Bluff where they would join Companies A and B and board a river boat for Memphis.

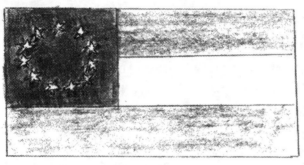 As they lined up, the ladies of El Dorado presented them with a new hand-made flag with three horizontal stripes, a red, white and another red, and a blue field in the upper left with eleven white stars in a circle. Then with the municipal band playing, they marched mostly out of step through town with young boys running along beside them and young ladies throwing flowers in their path. They were exhilarated.

On the dusty road toward Moro Bay the excitement began to wane and the high stepping began to slow. Someone near the front began to sing "Black Eyed Susan". Soon the entire company was engaged with Pickering's strong bass leading the others in the chorus which was somewhat on key. They were in high spirits but had about six days left to reach Pine Bluff.

That evening they camped on the banks of the Ouachita River where they would ferry across at daylight. Food rations were issued and Angus' group set about cooking black-eyed peas with fat back. It had been a long day and they turned in early. In no time it seemed the company bugle awakened them. It was a cool overcast morning and they shivered as they made weak coffee to drink with the morning issue of hardtack. The boys hesitatingly tasted hardtack for the first time and found the hard bread difficult to bite but hunger made the most of it.

An ancient man with a long beard ferried them across the river in three trips. They fell in for a long day's march with much less enthusiasm than the day before. The monotony was broken as they passed through the village of Hermitage where a small crowd gathered to cheer them on. Young women passed out tea cakes to the soldiers as they took a break. Several young men wanted to join their ranks but Captain Lacy told them that they would have to go through official channels.

They traveled a rutted road that was little more than a trail and sweated as the temperature hovered near 100 degrees with comparable humidity. The daily routine was repetitive but the adventurous spirits of the new recruits helped them take it all in stride. They passed through small settlements named Pansy, Calmer, and Friendship where they were cheered by locals gathered on the roadside.

Finally, exhausted, dirty and smelling of days without baths or clean clothes, they arrived at the outskirts of Pine Bluff.

Captain Lacy had them fall out while he went on to make contact with the other companies. The men sought the shade of large oaks where they sat or lay down while they talked of what was ahead.

There was a slough nearby and JC announced that he was going to take a bath. The water was muddy and seemed to be a host for snakes but as JC shucked his clothes others ran to join him. Yelling they jumped into the water and began to splash around. Even though the muddy water was warm, the wetness felt so good. Even McGoogan joined in the madness and they were still frolicking around when Captain Lacy returned and with a slight smile, sternly ordered them out and dressed to meet the rest of the Second Arkansas Infantry.

They tried to keep in step as they marched through downtown Pine Bluff. It was the biggest town that Angus had ever seen. There were stores on each side of the street some of them three or four stories high. The unpaved streets were lined with people cheering them on. Some of the kids ran into the street in their excitement and the marchers had to sidestep to avoid them. But the men were more interested in observing the young ladies dressed in their best hoop skirts and bonnets.

Company C soon arrived at March Landing where an old river boat was anchored waiting for boarding. Companies A and B were already there in loose formations. A tall thin scholarly looking man introduced himself as Major Bronaugh their commanding officer. As he looked out over the companies he told them that they were fine looking soldiers. Some of the other officers smiled at his remarks. The Major outlined their trip. They would board the boat for the trip down the Arkansas River to the Mississippi then up the river to Memphis. There they would board a train for the rest of the way to Virginia.

The boarding was chaotic as the three companies jockeyed for position on the gangplank. When they were finally aboard Angus joined his cooking group in the rear near the paddle wheel but did not join in the banter. He was feeling severe stomach pains. For two days as the boat made its way down the Arkansas and up the Mississippi, he lay on the deck with frequent trips to hang over the side of the boat for relief of his loose bowels. He did not eat the greasy food provided by the quartermaster so by the time they reached Memphis, he was feeling somewhat better.

About all they saw of Memphis were the rail yards as they were hurried aboard three flatbed rail cars and were soon on their way. As they traveled east, cotton fields gave way to more rugged terrain and finally Angus saw mountains for the first time. He felt a long way from home.

The slow moving train, with frequent stops to take on wood and water, took almost a week to reach Lynchburg, Virginia. On the way others of the group became sick with dysentery especially McGoogan and Keeling and both had not fully recovered when they reached Virginia.

They camped in a large field east of Lynchburg and a crusty old veteran of the Mexican War, Captain Jubal Jackson, was put in charge to make soldiers of them. He was relentless in his training. Captain Jackson first demanded that they make a column formation, stand at attention and march in step. As they grumbled and sweated, he had them marching long into the night. He instructed them how to take cover when attacked and assume defensive positions for returning fire. They practiced loading their rifles with gunpowder, patch, mini ball and ramming it home but not firing so as to avoid wasting ammunition. The captain instructed them to always aim low. Finally they were issued five rounds of ammunition for target practice. Most of them had been shooting all their lives and their accuracy surprised the Captain.

On the morning of the final presentation of colors, they were issued Confederate jackets though comparable pants were not available. They felt like real soldiers. Company C smartly marched around the field and presented arms to Major Bronaugh.  They were ready for their first assignment.

Angus now realized just how naive they were. They really had no idea of the coming battles.

REASSIGNMENT

The devastation of the battle at Beaver Dam Creek resulted in the formal disbanding of the 2nd Battalion. The 139 survivors were merged into the 3rd and continued throughout the war although many were soon discharged for various wounds and illnesses. Included in those discharged was Angus McKinnon. Many who were well enough to remain in service with the 3rd Arkansas would fall in the battles at Manassas, Gettysburg, Chickamauga, and the Wilderness. Only a dozen or so would survive to be surrendered at Appomattox Court House at the end of the war.

Angus joined the 8th Louisiana Infantry in hope of returning near home but the 8th went on to fight in the Army of Northern Virginia. They fought in the Battles of Manassas, Harpers Ferry, Antietam, Gettysburg, and other major campaigns.

CHAPTER 3

Angus enjoyed the cleanliness and food in the hospital but was beginning to get restless. The young lady that attended him that first day returned daily. Angus began to feel something special for her but she had little time to linger. On the fifth day he was able to get up and with a good bit of pain, began to walk around. He still had the mini-ball in his shoulder but the doctor did not seem inclined to remove it. After a week he felt ready to rejoin his buddies.

John Pickering returned in his boisterous way shouting, "Get off your ass and get moving."

He went on to report that JC was not doing well. He also reported that the remnant of the 2nd Regiment was to become part of the 3rd Regiment. So Angus would be joining other South Arkansas regulars as soon as he was fully recovered.

The day that Angus was released from the hospital, the commanding officer of the 3rd Regiment came by and told him that because of his wound, he would be discharged from the army.

Angus had mixed feelings. It would be great to get back home with his family but he was a thousand miles away. As Angus contemplated leaving the army, he reflected on what had happened while he was supposed to be actively engaged in the military action.

The 2ⁿᵈ Arkansas Infantry Battalion's first assignment was patrolling the south bank of the Potomac River guarding against a Yankee invasion. Bivouac had been miserable. The land was marshy so when it rained the water remained in huge puddles. Mosquitos tormented them until the weather turned cold and then they suffered from persistent rain and chill. Disease was rampant among Company C and more than half was admitted to the hospital where several died without ever seeing battle. Even Angus suffered from respiratory congestions and was in the hospital for a time.

The nights were long and boring when Angus was on patrol. Nothing ever seemed to happen. He could see the lights of his Yankee counterparts across the river but no contact was ever made. He again longed to see some action on the battlefield.

Then Angus was surprised and overjoyed when his older brother, Thomas, joined Company C. In June of 61, Thomas had joined the Three Creeks Mounted Rifles, which was part of the 1ˢᵗ Battalion and preceded Angus to Virginia. Thomas was six years older than Angus and had joined the army at his first opportunity. He was never happy farming and had much preferred reading a book to plowing a field. Even though he worked the farm of necessity, he wanted to be a school teacher. Thomas had been sick most of his time in service and when he petitioned his commander to join his brother, he was transferred.

The brothers' reunion was short lived. In just a few weeks, Thomas became seriously ill and was admitted to the hospital in Ashland. He died shortly thereafter. Angus had the lamentable job of writing his family of his brother's death.

After a miserable winter, the Battalion was ordered to Virginia to defend Richmond from the threat of attack by a large Union Army under the command of George B. McClellan. Spring was in the air and Company C was overjoyed to leave for a better climate.

Angus remembered his past excitement and anticipation of an actual battle. Now he knew the anguish of seeing his comrades falling. He'd had his fill of seeing their mangled bodies and was ready to get out.

He had a decision to make. He could begin the long journey home on his own or he could enlist in the 8th Louisiana and the army perhaps would send him back to Louisiana much closer to home.

Captain W. W. Brezeale of Company G, 8th Louisiana Infantry was looking for recruits because of casualties at Gains' Mill and Malvern Hill. Because he was under strength, he let it be known that he would accept those men discharged from the 3rd Arkansas Infantry who were only slightly wounded. Angus tried to talk others from the original 2nd Arkansas Infantry to join with him but found no takers.

There were a few members of Company G from north Louisiana but the majority were Cajun from south Louisiana. The Cajuns were different from any men that Angus had ever known. They were difficult to understand with their heavy accent and peculiar words. Moreover they were quick tempered, ready to take offence at any slight and tended toward violence. Angus was an outsider. He drifted to the few from north Louisiana with whom he had more in common. The Captain seeing the situation assigned Angus to tent with four privates from parishes that bordered Arkansas.

Angus made friends easily with his new companions. Their background in Northern Louisiana was very much like his own. His tent mates included the Lewis brothers, Americus and Simon. Their sandy hair and blue eyes made them attractive to the girls but they were very shy. Columbus Napoleon Butler, "Col", who was not so attractive, was constantly looking for women in the countryside. Louis Steele was the most serious soldier and tried only somewhat successfully to keep the others focused on their soldierly duties.

Company G was soon in action again. In August they engaged in skirmishes at Bristoe Station and Kettle Run. Angus and his tent mates were not involved as they were backup and did not make it to the front. The real fight came at the 2nd Battle at Manassas or Bull Run.

Company G under the command of Stonewall Jackson had orders to march north to confront General Pope who Lincoln had appointed to command the newly organized Army of Virginia after his disappointment with General McClellan. The ordinary soldier had no idea of the overall strategy but was only aware of long days' marches on thin rations. The hardtack and small portions of fatback were augmented by whatever the men could find on the road side. The countryside had been nearly stripped of provisions with the armies of both sides passing through. A night of celebration ensued when they made a rare find of a field of sweet potatoes.

Angus was bone weary. His shoes were coming apart and his pants were in bad repair. There was no occasion to bath and lice were a problem for all. When he could scrounge a piece of paper he would try to write a cheery letter home but it had been weeks since he last had heard from his family. He especially wanted to hear from Eliza Jane. At the age of seventeen, Angus had grown a scraggly beard that was the butt of numerous jokes from his tent mates. But despite the hardships they had developed a camaraderie that made it somewhat bearable.

Word filtered down that the forward troops of the 8th Regiment had a clash with Union forces but Company G was not involved so they settled down waiting further actions. Orders came soon enough. The Sergeant said that they would march around Pope's right flank to converge on the Union troops from the rear. So Company G joined the rest on a forced march over some 50 miles. Two days later with minimum effort they took Pope's supply depot at Manassas Junction. A day of wild feasting ensued.

Angus and his buddies stuffed themselves with canned roast beef, white bread, beans, and even cakes until they could eat no more. Some Federal officers' supply of fine whiskey was passed around but Angus had still not developed a taste for it. More meaningful to Angus was a new pair of boots. He also found himself a new pair of pants even though they were blue.

After his troops were satiated, Jackson ordered the Federal supplies burned and a move out to a more defensible position. They took up a position along an unfinished railroad cut near Manassas that offered considerable protection. Angus and his mates settled down with loaded weapons waiting for an inevitable attack. Rumors spread down the line that the Yankees were attacking with three times the number of Rebels. They knew that one Confederate was worth two Yankees but three?

Even though Angus thought that he was now a veteran, he felt panic when the Union cannons opened fire. The first shots went over their position but subsequent shots were coming closer. He heard screams down the line as cannons found their range. Then Angus saw blue hoards running toward them and he took aim and fired. A barrage of bullets met the oncoming Yankees and through a haze of gun smoke Angus saw many falling but others continued charging. To his right he was aware of blue fighters overrunning their position but shortly had to fall back. Again and again the union army attacked only to be hurled back.

Angus and his buddies were running out of ammunition and became exhausted from the continued onslaughts when darkness fell. The open area in their front was littered with the dead and wounded. Angus tried to close his ears to the agonizing cries of the dying. Confederate dead and wounded were taken from the defensive trench but the rest had to settle down in position for the night. After the carnage of the day, the still of the night seemed unreal. The stars overhead gave off a faint light and seemed to Angus to be unconcerned about what was happening below. Pickets were set while others slept fitfully. Near daybreak they became aware of voices to their rear and were soon relieved by welcomed reinforcements from General Longstreet's division.

Angus joined in cheering and dancing around when word came down that the Union Army had retreated back to Washington. But Angus felt uneasy. So many men had died for what? The Confederates had gained a small piece of land but the cost was so great. Would the cruel war go on until nobody was left?

Invasion of the North

Bolstered by success in the Seven Days Campaign and the 2nd battle of Manassas, Lee decided to take the fight to the North. Despite their successes he knew that his army's supplies were being depleted and the Union army was getting stronger. He reasoned that a victory in Union territory would give Northerners who were agitating for peace more support and would induce England and France to recognize the Confederacy and come to its aid. Moreover, he thought that Maryland as a slave state would welcome them and he would gain recruits and desperately need supplies. The people of Maryland did not respond as he anticipated.

Lee planned to invade Central Pennsylvania where a victory could end the war resulting in Southern independence. He realized that to secure his lines to the Shenandoah Valley, the source of much of his supplies, he would need to take out the Federal force at Harpers Ferry. So he temporarily divided his army by sending Jackson to take Harpers Ferry. Lee thought that McClelland would be slow to move out of Washington and that Jackson would be able to join him before they met Union opposition. But McClelland moved more quickly than anticipated and, aided by a Union soldier finding a carelessly lost copy of Lee's battle plan, threatened to engage the divided Army of Northern Virginia.

Jackson occupied the heights, encircling Harpers Ferry and easily occupied the arsenal capturing more than 12,500 Union prisoners. He then belatedly joined Lee in the Battle of Antietam or Sharpsburg.

The site of the battle was not planned by either side but that where the moving armies collided. September 7 proved to be the bloodiest day in the war with more than 22,000 casualties and 4,700 dead. The battle raged for three days in clashes at Miller's corn field, Dunker church, the sunken road, and the bridge across Antietam Creek. Neither army was able to overwhelm the other. Lee ended up withdrawing his battered army back across the Potomac. The first attempt to invade the North failed.

Chapter 4

The elation of victory at Manassas was short lived. Angus and his buddies had built a snug shelter of logs and canvas and had just settled in when word came down that they were on the move. This time they would be invading the North.

They were packing what meager supplies they had when shouts and cheers went up nearby. They soon joined in. Riding by on a large gray horse was General Robert E. Lee who they familiarly called, Bobby Lee. He rode straight in the saddle and had an air about him of quiet dignity. His presence renewed the enthusiasm of the men as destitute as they were.

Sergeant Herbert mustered Company G and announced that they would be marching under the command of Stonewall Jackson to Harpers Ferry to battle a Yankee garrison there.

Many of the men were barefoot with ragged uniforms and, as usual, hungry but spirits were high. As they moved into the upper reaches of the Shenandoah Valley they anticipated that more provisions would be found but both armies fighting around Winchester had left the area devastated. They continued on the barest rations of hard tack and small portions of fat back. Col constantly complained enough for them all but they grimly continued on. They saw some of their fellow soldiers primarily from Virginia fall out and slip through the forest on their way back home. The men of Company G were too far from home to consider desertion.

After a three-day miserable march they arrived on the heights overlooking Harpers Ferry. The view was beautiful. It was at the confluence of the Potomac and Shenandoah rivers. They could see the tiny town below with its military warehouses and Federal forces scurrying around as word had apparently reached them of the Rebel approach. Angus with the others sat down in the shade of several large oak trees waiting for the arrival of their cannons. It was the old military tradition of hurry up and wait.

Before sunup the following morning Angus heard the shouts and grunts as the cannons arrived and were put into place. As the day dawned bright and clear the cannons began firing on the Union placements. Angus watched the smoke rise from the devastation below. The scene fascinated him as long as he didn't think of the individual men being blown apart.

The men of Company G were at ease as the Confederate cannons continued shelling the Union positions below. Many of the men caught up on their sleep while others played cards or wrote letters that they hoped would somehow be delivered home. The officers let them rest until a fight broke among some of the card players, and consequently, they were ordered to fall in for practicing their marching maneuvers. The grumbling ended when they were ordered to march on Schoolhouse Ridge the only Union held high point overlooking Harper's Ferry.

But the battle never took place. Word came down that the Union commander saw the hopelessness of the situation, and waved the white flag. Angus thought that the report that more than 12,000 Union soldiers had been taken prisoner must be exaggerated but Sergeant Herbert swore that it was true. There was a windfall of captured Union supplies, but no time to enjoy them as word reached them that General Lee desperately needed them at a little town call Sharpsburg. So they again began an all-out march.

Angus was aware his the pitiful condition and that of men around him. Uniforms, if they could be called that, were ragged and many were barefoot. The men were gaunt from lack of food but hardened to military life and marched on with steadfast determination. Angus heard the rumbles of cannons and scattered musket fire as they approached Sharpsburg.

The 8th Louisiana was directed to join the Confederates in what the soldiers called West Woods. Angus and his group took defensive positions in the center of the Confederate line behind a series of rock formations. He nervously awaited the approach of Union troops that he could see moving through the old trees. On order they put down a withering fire.

Angus saw each end of the Confederate line close, threatening to engulf the Union attackers. So devastating were the converging volleys that in a matter of minutes half of the Union troops fell wounded or worse. In a panic the Union troops began a disorderly retreat. Sergeant Herbert ordered them to counterattack. Angus felt nauseated by the mangled bodies through which he had to maneuver.

The Rebels were reveling in their success but their elation was short-lived. As the Confederates charged out of the protective woods they met with the crossfire of dozens of Union cannons. Enemy cannon missiles wiped out swaths of attacking Confederates. All around Angus men were falling. Two of his tent mates just to his left fell mortally wounded. The Confederate charge staggered, gave way and moved back into defensive positions among the rock formations of the woods.

Angus was sickened by all the carnage. He just wanted to crawl in a hole to get away from it all. He once again wondered why civilized men were engaged in the killing of other human beings. But he kept his thoughts to himself.

Company G kept their position in the West Woods as the fighting shifted farther south. The noise of cannon and musket fire that came to them meant that a fierce battle was raging. After a short time Sergeant Hebert ordered them to march south to back up the precarious Confederate position on the sunken road. By the time they arrived the surviving soldiers had been forced to abandon it. Angus saw Union soldiers at the road's edge looking over piles of Confederate casualties.

The Confederates were now in full retreat. Their way back across the Potomac River was threatened when the Union soldiers took the bridge across Antietam Creek. But they were saved by the timely arrival of Hill's division up from Harpers Ferry.

It seemed to be a bedraggled and defeated army that went back across the Potomac. A slow rain was falling as the depleted army nursed its wounds back to Virginia. Angus, remarkably, was not wounded and tried to help his surviving tent mates who struggled to keep up. He learned that 103 men of Company G were killed or wounded.

It was somewhat surprising that the Union Army did not pursue and attack the weakened Confederates. But the Confederates were able to settle in near Winchester, attend their wounded, and go about recovering.

BACK TO VIRGINIA

After the retreat from Sharpsburg, the Army of Northern Virginia stopped at Winchester where Lee sought time to recuperate. McClellan rather than pressing the ragged Confederates set up camp only 20 miles away. He was so slow to move that Lincoln in exasperation replaced him as commander with Ambrose Burnside who was anxious to attack. He moved the Army of the Potomac southeast aiming to get between Lee and Richmond. He occupied the ground across the Rappahannock River from Fredericksburg. In the time it took to build pontoon bridges, Lee was able to occupy the heights across the river and a sunken road at it base.

The Union attack against the superior Confederate position was doomed to failure. Confederate cannons on the heights devastated the attacking Federals and the defensive position of the sunken road stopped the Union attacks again and again. Union losses were more than 12,000 when Burnside moved his army out. Lee is reported to have remarked that "It is well that war is so terrible else we would become too fond of it."

Both armies went into winter encampments. The Confederates especially suffered with lack of supplies and rampant diseases. In the meantime Lincoln had once again replaced the Union commander. "Fighting Joe Hooker" was the new hope to at last defeat Lee and the Army of Northern Virginia. In the spring of 1863 with far superior numbers, Hooker made an elaborate plan to surround Lee, but a flanking move by Stonewall Jackson doomed him to failure at Chancellorsville. Once again the brilliant leadership of Lee won the day but Jackson was wounded by mistake by his own men and later died. It would prove to be a devastating loss for the Confederates.

Hooker's lack of success led to his dismissal and the appointment of George G Meade to lead the Union Army of the Potomac.

CHAPTER 5

Angus was tired of war. His shoulder often ached, he was always hungry, he struggled with body lice, and his uniform was in shambles. He hadn't had a letter from home in months. He thought of the serenity of home with his family around him. He remembered the clean and beautiful Liza Jane and fervently hoped that she would still be there when, if ever, he returned. But the war went on.

The Army of Northern Virginia was encamped for six weeks and the soldiers began to recover. A bit more food was coming to them from the lower Shenandoah Valley and the weather was mostly good. Only Angus and Col were left of the original tent group so they were joined by three others who were far less amicable. Two of the new mates were constantly searching for whatever alcohol they could buy or steal. Col was recovering from a wound to his lower right leg so Angus helped him maneuver around. Consequently they pretty much stayed to themselves.

The settled life of the 8th Louisiana came to an abrupt halt when word came down that they were to make a hurried march east to the small town of Fredericksburg. They were told that the Yankees were under a new commander who was attempting to surround them and cut them off from Richmond. Once again it was a harrowing march and they took up a position behind a ridge south of Fredericksburg and waited the Yankee attack. Their unit was in reserve behind the front line. It was December now and the day was cold and foggy. About midmorning the sun came out and they heard the cannon bombardment begin with steady musket fire.

Angus had settled down with others waiting for orders when they heard the noise of the battle move closer. They were ordered to move to the front line where the Union troops had briefly broken through but the withering rebel fire sent them scurrying back and it seemed that the battle moved farther west. The 8th was without any casualties.

The sounds of battle continued all day at what they later learned was Marye's Heights and the sunken road. A slightly wounded soldier who was sent to the rear was anxious to tell what was happening. Angus and his comrades gathered around him as he described the slaughter. Wave after wave of Union soldiers attacked and were beaten back with minimum Rebel casualties. He vividly told of the attackers bodies piled on the field approaching the sunken road. There were so many dead Union soldiers that it was said one could cross the field stepping from body to body without ever touching the ground.

As night came, the battle lulled and the field grew almost quiet. A story circulated that one Confederate soldier couldn't stand the pitiful cries of the Union wounded and circulated among them giving water to the dying. The next day the Union Army, thoroughly defeated, left the field and moved back across the Rappahannock River.

Both armies settled into winter quarters as the weather turned miserable. Food for the Confederate soldiers was meager. Blankets were thin if available at all. The cold wet weather continued.

CONFEDERATE'S COSTLY SUCCESS

President Lincoln continued efforts to find a general who could successfully lead the Army of the Potomac. He had gone through a secession of generals from Irvin McDowell, George B. McClellan, John Pope, Ambrose E Burnside, and finally Joseph Hooker seeking the one who could at last defeat the Confederate Army of Northern Virginia. Each had superior numbers and resources but were no match for Robert E. Lee.

Lee's bedraggled army met a larger Union force first at Fredericksburg and then at Chancellorship with spectacular success. Even though Robert E. Lee's army never lost a battle in Virginia until the end at Petersburg and Appomattox, each engagement left his army weaker while the Federals steadily became stronger.

Lee's primary hope was to continue until pressure from Northerners seeking to end the war were successful or European Nations would come to the Confederate's aid. Neither came about.

CHAPTER 6

Spring in 1863 came as a welcome change from the harsh winter. The Confederate soldiers still lacked basic supplies, but the warmth and renewal of the earth made them almost cheerful. Angus basked in the warm sun and thought of home where it would be planting season. The sergeant had them doing drills but he was not demanding and they were somewhat half-hearted.

Near the end of April the 8th Louisiana was ordered to move out to face a new Federal threat. Angus' friend Col was an incessant talker who moved about the regiment and brought news back to his platoon whether it was true or not. He announced to the gathered group that the Union had a new general, "Fighting Joe Hooker," who aimed to take Richmond. Hooker had an overwhelming force and he vowed to crush Lee's army.

The major confrontation was taking place at a crossroad called Chancellorsville. However the 8th Louisiana, under the command of General Jubal Early, was to take a position at Fredericksburg to check the movement of the Federal garrison there. Angus and his immediate unit took a defensive position on the southern section end of the Rebel line that was attempting to hold the opposing Union forces from joining their main unit farther west.

Angus stoically took a defensive position. He heard the sound of cannons and musket fire down the line but saw no action at his front. Then the order came down to move as rapidly as possible to reinforce Lee's position at Chancellorsville. After a hurried march, they arrived at a furious battle taking place at tiny community called Salem's Church north of the major confrontation at Chancellorsville. Angus' unit arrived to reinforce the Confederate division there but the tide was already turning in their favor.

The Union force shortly thereafter retreated, leaving Salem Church. Hooker's vaulted army was withdrawing back across the Rappahannock River. The elation of victory was cut short when word filtered down that Stonewall Jackson had been fatally wounded. Angus had been under the command of Jackson at the battle of Harper's Ferry but had actually never seen him but admired his accomplishments. Jackson's daring maneuverings that played a major part in Confederate victories would be sorely missed. Lee mourned the loss of "his right arm."

Angus and his company settled down again near Fredericksburg in the aftermath and received food and some supplies captured from the retreating Federals. But full provisions were sorely needed. Angus had boots that he jealously guarded as many of his comrades were barefooted. More ammunition was distributed and they were soon on the march again.

GETTYSBURG

Lee's success at Fredericksburg and Chancellorsville, despite his inferior numbers and supplies, led to the decision to once again attempt an invasion of the North. His reasoning was much the same as his earlier effort but the situation was more desperate. Lee needed a victory in Northern territory and hopefully a rapid end to the war.

As Lee's army marched through Maryland and into Pennsylvania it was described as a motley crew. Half of the men were barefoot, wore mismatched and patched uniforms, and sported few hats. They were constantly hungry and scavenged the roadsides for food. But their spirits were high and their recent success filled them with confidence.

The Union Army was once again under a new commander, General George G Meade. He was not the risk-taker of Hooker or Burnside but a methodical solid leader.

Because the Confederate cavalry under J. E. B. Stuart was away making daring raids on Union supply lines, Lee was not sure where the adversaries were and rather stumbled upon Meade's army at the little village of Gettysburg. Meade occupied the hills to the east. Mindful of the success that the Rebel forces had had with flanking movements, Meade fortified his left and right with extra forces. Confederates attacked the larger forces from the west and north.

The battle raged for three days with first one side having success and then the other. Although outnumbered, Lee was desperate for victory and realized that Meade had his flanks heavily fortified. Against the advice of James Longstreet, he launched a frontal attack on the center of the Union position. Led by General George C. Pickett's Virginia division, the attacker's met massed artillery and infantry fire. The attack was doomed. Although the Rebels in a final push penetrated the Union line they were quickly pushed back and virtually destroyed.

The battered army of Northern Virginia withdrew back across the Potomac. Once again the two armies faced each other along the Rappahannock River. Confederate casualties were some 28,000, more than a third of Lee's army. Union casualties were approximately 23,000. Although Lee's army would continue for almost two years and experienced a number of victories, it was never the same.

CHAPTER 7

Word filtered down that they were to invade the North. Angus questioned whether they had the necessary equipment or able men to make the move but he just followed orders.

The 8th Louisiana was once again were on the march into Maryland. Food was scarce and they scrounged whatever they could find along the way. Civilians in the towns and farms hid from them and only the children came out to watch their passing. The reputation of the "Louisiana Tigers" as a violent group preceded them.

Angus did not participate with the men that went on night raids to steal chickens or pigs but joined, when allowed, in eating the plunder. He was more likely to go into fields of corn and eat the young ears raw. The weary soldiers continued the march into Pennsylvania without contact with the enemy until they reached the little town of Gettysburg.

Angus could hear the boom of cannon and rattle of musket fire as they approached from the west but they were ordered to settled down in reserve. Medical orderlies bringing wounded to the rear reported the Confederates were taking the town and the Union Army had taken to the hill east of town.

After a troubled night Angus was awakened and after a piece of hardtack without coffee, was ordered to prepare for battle. His unit marched out the face the Federal forces on what was known as Cemetery Hill. Union cannons on the heights were wreaking havoc on the arriving Confederate forces. Captain Hebert hastily ordered attack and with a rebel yell the Rebels charged the hill. They were under the range of the cannons but musket fire from the infantry on the hill raked the charging Confederates. The flag bearer was knocked down and Angus rushed to pick it up but a fellow soldier beat him to it. The new flag bearer lasted only a few minutes before he too was down. The momentum of the charging Rebels carried them to the top where they captured several cannons.

Their success was short lived. Union reinforcements rushed them and they were forced back with heavy losses. Somehow Angus survived among the many wounded and dead as they, in wild disorder, retraced their steps down the hill.

The 8th Louisiana once again encamped west of town to nurse their wounds and get ready for further battle. After catching his breath, Angus spent time helping to bandage the wounds of the less serious casualties. The sounds of battle continued unabated. Later in the day they were ordered to prepare to move out to support the Confederate movements in the south but night came without their engagement.

The third day dawned with bright sunshine and there were sounds of mass movements of Confederate troops. Angus' unit joined the gathering as they prepared for a major charge into the center of the Federal line on top of Cemetery Ridge for an all-or-nothing push to win the battle. Angus' unit was stationed near the rear for reinforcement and he could see the entire battle unfold. The ensuing conflict that later became known as Pickett's Charge was a resounding defeat for the Rebels as they never made it to the top of the ridge.

Angus saw scores of his fellow soldiers fall as the attack faltered and began to retreat. He could see that fewer than half of the attackers were returning. The carnage was overwhelming. He would never forget the devastation and despaired of the continued war. Why couldn't they just quit?

Lee gathered the vestige of his army and began the long march back south. Lee's army limped along and they were fortunate the Federals did not pursue. Angus trudged along in as daze just managing to put one foot in front the other.

Nearing the End

The 8th Louisiana Infantry continued to be a part of all the decisive battles in Virginia. In most of these battles Lee's army held its own or was victorious but steadily grew weaker while Grant's army gained strength.

There were a number of battles in which the 8th Louisiana played a role. In the fall of 1863 the two armies thrust back and forth across the Rappahannock River with neither making much headway. A major clash occurred at Rappahannock Station in which they, under the command of Jubal Early, engaged in brutal hand-to-hand combat. One hundred sixty-two of the 8th Louisiana were captured. Both armies went into winter quarters where the Confederates especially suffered from lack of basic necessities.

In the spring of 1864 the war became even bloodier. Ulysses S. Grant was now appointed to lead the Union forces. A second Battle of the Wilderness took place in early May with heavy casualties on both sides. The tangled forest caught fire and hundreds of wounded on the battlefield were cremated. At Spotsylvania the Confederate defenses at the Mule Shoe were the sight of fierce fighting that left the field piled high with wounded and dead but no clear victor. Cold Harbor was a resounding Confederate victory but Lee's army was so depleted that all he could do was try to stay between Grant and Richmond.

Grant continued pounding the Confederate defenses. Lee's army took a last stand at Petersburg near Richmond where they dug in with multiple lines of trenches and resisted repeated attacks. A well-equipped Union army maintained a siege throughout the winter and early spring. In a bizarre move the Union commanders used coal miners from Pennsylvania to dig tunnels under the Confederate defenses and set dynamite to explode the Rebel line. Even though the forward Confederate defenses were destroyed, the attacking Federals were caught in the crater and suffered heavy losses. The siege continued.

By April 1965, Lee's defense was broken by a heavy bombardment of the strengthening Union Army and Lee fled with what was left of his troops to the southwest hoping to make a stand in a better defensible position. But they were overtaken and surrounded at Appomattox Court House where on Palm Sunday Lee surrendered. The war was over.

Chapter 8

Angus sat on a dirt mound with Petersburg at his back. He could hear the noise of battle that was constant every day. There were always casualties. The pitiful remnant of Lee's Army of Northern Virginia was pinned down in trenches surrounding Petersburg. Angus' clothes were in rags and his shoes were held together with string. He was gaunt from months of constant hungry and had not eaten in three days. The trenches that were now his home were filthy. He could not escape the stench. When it rained, and that was often, the trenches became a muddy quagmire but the Rebels risked being the target of snipers if they climbed out.

It was summer again after a miserable winter and spring but there was little joy in it. Angus was numb from three years of war. He just didn't care anymore. But he roused himself out of habit whenever called to the forward trenches to fire on the Yankee attackers. The Rebel soldiers were given only 18 rounds and when these were expended they had to be ready for hand-to-hand combat.

The last two years seemed like an eternity. The battles all ran together and Angus had trouble differentiating among them. The horror of the dead and maimed in the chaos of bursting shells and thick musket fire was almost unbearable. He fired, reloaded, advanced or retreated, all on automation. Even though almost of his tent mates had been wounded, killed, or captured, somehow he endured. Angus had ceased praying moments before battle. At times he wished that he too could join his fallen comrades. But the unconscious will to survive kept him going.

The days and weeks between battles were as bad. Hunger was constant. The men built makeshift shelters with whatever scraps were at hand. However the winter wind and snow could not be kept out. The countryside had been fought over so much that it was mostly barren. Oh, if only he could go home.

After the withdrawal from Gettysburg, Angus felt that the war was lost. He barely escaped capture at Rappahannock Station when 162 of the 8th Louisiana Infantry were captured. Even though Confederates held their ground at the battle of the wilderness and Spotsylvania and had an overwhelming victory at Cold Harbor, they were bloodied and weakened beyond repair.

Angus could not escape the horror that filled his mind. He could still smell the smoke from the fires at the Wilderness that burned the helpless wounded. He could still see the bodies piled high at the battle of the Mule Shoe at Spotsylvania. He could still hear the cries of the fallen Yankees at Cold Harbor. Yet the war went on.

Angus was once again about to follow orders to move to the front when a loud explosion sent men and cannons skyward. Dust and smoke whirled around him. The First Sergeant shouted, "All men to the front."

As the dust began to settle Angus saw a large crater below with Yankees flooding in and the Rebels rushing to the rim. Leading the charge below was a division of newly organized colored soldiers. The Sergeant commanded that they fire and Angus with the others began firing at the helpless victims below. They were mowed down like a scythe cutting wheat. After the initial surge the Yankees retreated and a rebel yell rang round the defenders but Angus only felt despair.

Angus later learned from others that Pennsylvania coal miners had dug tunnels beneath Confederate lines and set explosives. When they were detonated, forward Rebels line were destroyed but the attacking Yankees were not able to take advantage and the stalemate went on.

The siege of Petersburg continued with Grant applying unrelenting pressure. Winter came early and hard. The Confederates' condition reached new heights of misery. They built lean-tos from whatever materials they could find or dug mud caves to the rear. The cold was unremitting and shipments of food from Richmond were few and far between.

With spring of 1865, Grant unleashed a concentrated attack that broke through the thin Rebel lines. Angus hastily joined the remnants of Lee's army retreating to the southwest. He was exhausted and blindly followed the man in front him. They were under constant attack and when they staggered into the little village of Appomattox Court House, the Union Army was on all sides. Word came down that Lee had found no alternative but surrender. After stacking their weapons,

Angus and the men around him went into mourning mixed with relief. Could the war be over?

After the surrender, General Lee emerged from the old farm house, mounted his horse, and rode before his men. The exhausted men stood and removed their hats. Lee's farewell statement to his men was dignified and touching. He stated:

"With an unceasing admiration of your constancy and devotion to your Country, and grateful remembrance of your kind and generous consideration of myself, I bid you all an affectionate farewell. You will take with you the satisfaction that proceeds from the consciousness of duty faithfully performed and I earnestly pray that a merciful God will extend to you His blessings and protection."

Angus was surprised at the generosity of the Federals. The former Confederates were given food and transportation as far as it was available to their homes.

AFTERMATH

After Appomattox, fighting was soon over in other parts of the south. With the cessation of hostilities, those that survived often had long journeys home. Most transportation systems had been destroyed in the fighting so that few trains or river boats were left and consequently the main method of travel left was walking. Former Confederate soldiers, in tatters and constantly hungry, were seen on the roads and byways trudging back home. They had no money and after their meager supplies given by the Federals was exhausted, depended on people along the way for sustenance.

The eighth Louisiana Infantry had to travel from Virginia back to Louisiana and the trip took several weeks. They traveled through devastated countryside often found civilians in worse shape than themselves. Rivers was about the only reliable source of travel if they could find a boat that would take them without pay.

Once they arrived back home, they were likely to find the homestead damaged or destroyed so that getting back to normal was problematic. This coupled with the emotional residue of war made relationships with the remaining family difficult.

CHAPTER 9

Angus started the long journey home on foot with just his bed roll and a few days of food allotted to the former Confederates by their Yankee capturers. He was in a group of about 12 others mainly from Northern Louisiana. Their clothes were in bad repair and some did not even have shoes. But they felt free from the daily horrors of war. Some talked incessantly about home but Angus remained quiet. He couldn't quite grasp that the battles were over and he would soon see the fields of home.

They walked to Lynchburg hoping to catch a train south but the rails were torn up and they were told that the nearest functioning train was 60 more miles at Roanoke. The group passed through a devastated country side. Angus saw many burned out houses surrounded by fields that were overgrown. Destitute families silently watched them pass by and some bedraggled children fearfully followed in their wake. One obviously hungry little boy bravely asked Angus for food. Angus hesitated a moment before reaching into his pack for a hard biscuit. The little boy grabbed it from his hand and ran, perhaps thinking that another kid might try to take it from him.

When the group reached Roanoke they found a working train and boarded a flatbed car taking them to Memphis. As Angus road along, he was reminded of the trip in the opposite direction that he had made along the same track four years earlier. He felt old and used up.

Memphis was a madhouse. The streets were filled with newly freed colored who wandered around not knowing what to do. Smooth talking Carpetbaggers were ready to take advantage wherever they could. Some of the more belligerent Southerners were recruiting for a newly organized group that they called the KKK. Angus and his fellow war veterans wandered through the crowds only seeking a way home.

They went down to the riverfront looking for a boat going south. They, of course, had no money and were turned away until they met a sympatric owner of a dilapidated old river boat. He said that they could earn their fare by working to load supplies headed for a Federal garrison in Shreveport. He provided them with meager food and allowed them to sleep below deck with the crew. It was a bare existence but they were elated to see home in sight.

Soldier's Heart

Soldiers engaged in the civil suffered the after affects as they do in all wars. Doctors at the time termed it "Soldier's Heart." It was thought to be as physical condition connected to a rapid beating heart. Symptoms as recorded included bizarre gaits, paralysis, muteness, shaking, and sometimes seizures. It has since been determined to be primarily a psychological condition.

In later wars it became known as shell shock, battle fatigue, combat fatigue, and most recently as PDST. Soldiers returning from Iraq and Afghanistan suffer from apathy, alienation, depression, and restlessness. They experience nightmares, reaction to sudden loud noise, flashbacks to battle scenes, and avoidance of social engagements. They are usually unable to talk of the experience.

Recovery is difficult and some never make it. Many turn to drugs or alcohol to dull the pain. Tragically, some take their own life. At best, recovery takes time. It is crucial to have the understanding of those closest to them.

Angus most likely suffered but his subsequent history indicate that he fully recovered.

CHAPTER 10

Angus trudged along a rutted dirt road as he entered South Arkansas only a few miles from home. He was bone weary after three weeks of trying by any means to find his way back home. He was, as always, hungry, in rags that stank to high heavens. Still infested with body lice, he limped along a dirt road. Angus saw with dismay empty weed-filled fields of neighbors that were stands of corn and cotton when he left home a lifetime ago.

As Angus entered the lane that led to his familiar dogtrot home, he saw his mother struggling to plow the south field with a scrawny mule. His little sister, Amanda, digging in the dirt in the front yard. As he approached she looked up and with a startled cry ran into the house. Angus' father came to the door in a night shirt carrying the old shotgun. He could barely stand.

He weakly said, "Leave us alone. We have no food."

Angus threw his hands wide and said, "Daddy, it's me."

The old man paused, squinted his eyes and cried, "Son, we thought you were dead. Come to me."

Angus hobbled up the front steps and for the first time in his life, embraced his father. His father turned to Amanda and said, "Run to your mother and tell her that Angus is back home."

It was a joyous reunion. Amanda was sent to unharness the mule and take him back to the barn. His mother took Angus and his father into the kitchen and had them sit down while she busied herself with cooking.

Angus' parent talked of what had happened at home while Angus was away. Even though the war had not penetrated western Union County, they had been profoundly affected. Some basics such as coffee, sugar and salt were no longer available. Salt was especially important since it was used to cure the meat of butchered hogs. The market for cotton had dried up so that there was no ready money even if these supplies were to be had.

Foraging parties regularly came through the neighborhood not from the Union Army but the Confederate. At first the farmers gave gladly to support their cause but later the army began to take necessities. Most of their stock of corn, all their chickens, cows, and pigs were taken except for one lone hog they managed to hide in the Corney Creek bottom.

They scraped the ground in the smoke house and salvaged some salt for curing the pork so that when they butchered the hog they could save part of it. The rest they traded or gave to neighbors. Old man LaGrone had saved his chickens and traded a rooster and two hens for a side of bacon. Another neighbor traded a bucket of sorghum syrup for a fresh ham. So they had made it through the winter but their supply of corn meal was running out and spring planting was most important.

Their backdoor garden provided a variety of vegetables throughout the summer but winters were hard.

They had turned to trapping and hunting to provide for the table. Angus' father had built traps for rabbits and was successful from time to time. He hunted squirrels until ammunition for his old shotgun ran short.

Amanda had also helped out. She roamed the woods and picked huckleberries, blackberries, possum grapes and muscadines when they were is season.

Angus' father had contracted what they thought was pneumonia last winter and nearly died but was slowly recovering. Consequently his mother was struggling to plow and plant the field.

Angus listened to their accounts but when asked about the war, he struggled silently and finally said, "I just can't talk about it. It's just too much," as he struggled to restrain tears. He had thought that he was no longer capable of crying.

As he sat there Angus became intensely aware of his filthy state and stated the he was going to the creek to bath. His mother handed him a bar of lye soap and clothes that he had left behind when he went off to war. Angus waded into the muddy water and began to scrub himself until his skin was raw but he knew that he'd never get rid of the smell of war.

Angus sat on the side of the creek letting the sun dry him and dressed. The clothes hung on his gaunt figure. He had grown taller in the past four years but not filled out as would be expected. He felt that he could never be the same person that he had been when he last wore these clothes.

The next morning, Angus woke in a cold sweat. At first he didn't know where he was. He still heard the explosions of cannon shell, the screams of comrades mangled as a result, the acrid smells of gunpowder, the piles of bodies cut down, and the vivid fear he felt in the midst of  battle. He couldn't go back to sleep and slipped outside to watch the sun come up.

It was Sunday and his mother urged him to dress for church but Angus couldn't face it. He sat on the front steps as the family wagon drove off. Angus couldn't muster any enthusiasm when his mother told him that everybody at church had asked about him. Even Eliza Jane had inquired as to when she would see him.

Angus' mother talked to the preacher about his lack of interest in anything. The preacher said, "Angus' condition is not unusual. Many returning soldiers who have been in battle show the symptoms. It is called "Soldier's Heart" and it usually fades over time. Let him recover at his own pace."

In the weeks that followed, Angus plowed the fields, planted corn, and helped his mother plant the garden. His dad was slowly recovering but still couldn't muster energy to do much. At the end of long days of hard work Angus felt better but the nightmares continued and he still could not talk about the war and refused to see other people. He often had flashbacks of horrific scenes. He was unable to forget.

When the Keeling family came for a Sunday afternoon visit, Angus hid in the barn. He was sitting on a bale of hay when Eliza Jane timidly looked in. There was a long pause. Angus couldn't look at her.

With a deep breath she said, "I've been wondering when I would see you."

Angus looked up at her and was awed by her fresh beauty. He looked down and said, "I guess I can't get over the war."

Eliza Jane sat down beside him and quietly said, "You don't have to hurry it."

Angus felt strangely comforted. They sat without talking until Eliza Jane's mother called her to go home. She lightly touched Angus on the shoulder as she left him.

Angus gradually began to feel better. He went to church where he would see Eliza Jane. After a few weeks, they sat together. It was a lengthy courtship and finally in 1866 he asked her to marry him.

With the help of their parents, they bought a forty-acre farm, built a small house, and began a fruitful life together. Despite his happiness, the mini ball in his shoulder remained a constant reminder of the war.

Post Script

Angus returned home where he courted and married Eliza Jane Keeling in 1866. Even with the mini ball still in his shoulder, he became a successful farmer. He fathered twelve children of which ten survived to adulthood. Angus died in 1899 at the age of 55 and was buried at old Scotland Cemetery near Junction City, Arkansas. Eliza Jane applied for and received a widow's pension of $50 in 1901 for Angus' service in the Confederate Army.

Apparently his children remained a close family. They erected a large monument for his grave, likely several years later, replacing the original marker. A sentiment on the monument reads,

"A light from our household is gone

A voice we love is still

A place is vacant in our hearts

That can never be filled"

In 1925 his descendants inaugurated a family reunion. The McKinnon Reunion is celebrated on the first Sunday in June each year and continues to this day.

Bridge over Antietam Creek

Confederate position at Battle of Fredericksburg Sunken Road

Battle at Antietam

Battle of Beaver Dam Creek

Battle at Cold Harbor

Bloody Angle Battle of Spotsylvania Court House

Printed in the United States
By Bookmasters